NOAH'S ROCKET

by
TONY FRAIS

Illustrations by Rosalind Wilson

Published in 2004 by Anthony T. FRAIS,
9 Sandhill Oval, LEEDS LS17 8EB
UNITED KINGDOM
afrais@tiscali.co.uk
REPRINT WITH ADDITIONS
2005

ISBN   0 9548068 0 8

Acknowledgements

Many thanks to:
Helen
Deborah
Micky
Noah
Pat

*The children of
Fir Tree Primary School, Leeds*

Do you know the story of Noah's Ark, which happened a long, long time ago?

Have you ever wondered what might have happened to Noah if he was living today?

This is the story about Noah and his amazing adventure, a story that happened not so very long ago . . .

CHAPTER 1

Noah was a good man. He was a very kind and polite man.

He lived with his wife Ethel in a small house in London. His three sons, Ben, Joseph and David and their wives would come to visit him. It made Noah very happy that his family came to see him.

But Noah was not always very happy. He had noticed that some people were not very kind or polite and that the world was becoming a very dangerous place.

However, Noah was not the only one to be unhappy. Somebody,

and this was a really big somebody, was also very unhappy with things . . .

One day, Noah was having a little walk around his back garden. Suddenly, he heard a large *whooshing* sound and then someone's voice talking to him.

"HELLO NOAH."

"Who is that?" asked Noah, as he tried to find out where the voice was coming from.

"THIS IS GOD SPEAKING TO YOU. THE WORLD HAS BECOME A VERY BAD PLACE WITH TOO MANY WICKED PEOPLE.

I AM GOING TO DESTROY THEM BY CAUSING A GIANT FLOOD.

I WILL MAKE IT RAIN FOR FORTY DAYS AND FORTY NIGHTS.

ALONG WITH YOUR FAMILY AND YOURSELF, I WILL SAVE OTHER GOOD PEOPLE, BUT YOUR SPECIAL TASK IS TO SAVE THE ANIMALS.

NOAH, YOUR GARDEN IS TOO SMALL TO BUILD A VERY LARGE ARK OR A VERY LARGE SUBMARINE. YOU ONLY HAVE ENOUGH SPACE TO BUILD SOMETHING VERY TALL INSTEAD!

NOAH, I WANT YOU TO BUILD A GIANT SPACE ROCKET.

BUILD IT 180 METRES HIGH.

TAKE YOUR WIFE, YOUR THREE SONS AND THEIR WIVES AND PUT THEM INTO THE ROCKET. ALSO, YOU WILL COLLECT TWO OF EVERY LIVING CREATURE, MALE AND FEMALE, AND PUT THEM, WITH ENOUGH FOOD FOR EVERYONE, INTO THE ROCKET."

"Is someone playing a trick on me?" shouted Noah.

The voice went on.

"YOU WILL BLAST OFF AND GO INTO ORBIT AROUND THE EARTH UNTIL YOU KNOW IT IS SAFE TO COME BACK.

NOAH, YOU ARE THE MAN I HAVE CHOSEN TO HELP ME TO MAKE THE WORLD A BETTER PLACE.

NOW GET ON WITH YOUR TASK!"

WHOOSH!

Noah kept looking around his garden hoping to find the person who had been talking to him. But he couldn't see anybody and thought that perhaps he was going completely potty.

Noah went inside his house and called to his wife.

"Ethel, when I was in the garden just now, God spoke to me. He said that he is going to make a giant flood and destroy all the bad people in the world. But he wants me to save the animals. I've got to build a space rocket tall enough to take you with the kids and their wives and a male and female of all the creatures in the world. Everyone has to come with me into the rocket. Then we blast off into orbit. He told me that I have been chosen as a very special person and, when we come back, I then have to help Him make the world a better place."

Ethel told Noah that he should see a doctor about hearing this mysterious voice that was telling him to do some very strange things.

But for some reason that he could not explain, Noah began to believe that it really was God that had spoken to him, and there was nothing left to do but get on with what he needed to do . . .

CHAPTER 2

Noah started to collect the parts he needed to build the rocket. He collected lots of scrap metal from the scrap metal yard and made a big pile of it in his garden. Then he needed to find some rocket engines. Noah thought that the best place to go for rocket engines might be a shop selling odd things that nobody had any use for. He remembered that he had seen that sort of shop only a few streets away from the scrap yard. Noah got into his car and drove down to the shop.

He went into the shop and was greeted by a salesman who was wearing the whitest suit that Noah had ever seen. Noah asked him if by any chance he had any unwanted space rocket engines.

"I've got two massive ones at the back that nobody wants because they are far too big and far too powerful. I'd be very pleased if you would take them away," said the salesman.

"I'd be happy to," said Noah. "How much will that be?"

"Oh you can have them for nothing!" replied the salesman.

"That's wonderful," replied Noah, "thank you very much indeed."

The salesman helped Noah to strap the rocket engines to the top of his car and wished him good luck. As Noah drove home, he thought how lucky he was to get exactly what he needed – that salesman must have been an angel!

The next day, Noah started to build the rocket in his back garden.

After a few weeks, the rocket had reached a height of 100 metres – tall enough to be seen by everybody in the area. Noah's next-door neighbour, who had been watching all this going on, called up to him.

"Just what do you think you're playing at Noah?"

Noah shouted back, "There's going to be a big flood. I have been especially chosen by God to build a space rocket. I have to take my family and a male and female of every kind of animal into the rocket and blast off into orbit around the world until it is safe to come back again."

Noah's neighbour replied that he thought Noah was completely potty and that he must stop building the rocket because it was making the picture on his television set go all wobbly. Noah took no notice and day after day the rocket grew taller and taller.

As Noah's rocket grew taller and taller, all of the neighbours started to get wobbly pictures on their television sets. They called the police and asked them to have a word with Noah.

The next morning, a policeman arrived in Noah's back garden. The policeman called up to Noah and told him that if he did not dismantle the rocket, he would be arrested. Noah shouted back that, as God had told him to do it, he could not stop building the rocket. That was enough for the policeman.

"Come down now Noah! You are under arrest!"

Noah came down and the policeman took him down to the police station to be charged with being a nuisance.

After charging Noah, the policeman told him that he must take the rocket down because, if he didn't, he would be arrested again. Noah tried to explain that he couldn't do that.

"I must finish the rocket and collect a male and female of all the animals, and put them inside. Then we can blast off into orbit around the earth. You won't have any more trouble from me after that."

The policeman had heard enough.

"That's enough about all this nonsense. I'm going to have to lock you up." The policeman took Noah downstairs, put him in a room, and told him that if he promised not to go on building the rocket he could go home.

Ethel came down to see Noah at the police station.

"You'd better do as the police tell you Noah, or they won't let you out. You'll come home and forget about all this nonsense about the rocket and the animals."

Ethel kissed him goodbye and went home. Noah thought that even if he escaped from the police station, how was he going to build a rocket without getting into trouble with the police again? Somehow he had to build his rocket without anyone knowing about it.

"How do you hide a 180 metre-tall rocket?" thought Noah. "I will just have to find a way. Somehow, I must do what God has told me to do."

CHAPTER 3

The next morning, a different policeman came to see Noah. The first thing Noah noticed was that the policeman's uniform wasn't blue. It was a very bright white.

Noah was reminded of the salesman who gave him the rocket engines. He too was wearing a very bright white suit.

"Noah," said the policeman, "you can go home and do what you must do."

The policeman wished Noah good luck. Noah was grateful and happy that he was going home, but he was still very worried about how he was going to build a rocket without being arrested again. He arrived home from the police station to a very surprised Ethel.

"Ethel," said Noah, "a policeman has told me to come home and get on with what I must do. That means I must somehow build another rocket."

This did not make Ethel very happy!

"There is going to be trouble if you carry on with this. Anyway, some men came and dismantled the rocket. They have taken all the metal away and they're coming back to take away the rocket engines next week, so you can forget all about this silly idea."

Although Noah was very upset that the rocket had been taken away, at least he still had the rocket engines. But how was he supposed to build another rocket before the men came back to take the engines away? How could he build another rocket without anybody noticing?

"I've not done very well," he cried. "What am I going to do now?"

CHAPTER 4

The next morning, a very worried and upset Noah walked into the city trying to think about what to do next. As he turned a corner, he suddenly saw a building he had never seen before. Not only was it a very tall building, it was also a very unusual shape. Noah went over to it and noticed that it was a multi-storey office block.

"I wonder how tall it is?" thought Noah, as he slowly stepped backwards to see the top of the building. "What an unusual shape for an office block; it looks like a giant cucumber!" As Noah stepped back to see the top of the building, he bumped into a man wearing a very bright white suit.

"Sorry about that," said Noah to the man.

"That's alright!" said the man. "No harm done. Admiring the building are you?"

"I am," said Noah. "It's a very unusual building; I've never seen anything like it. It looks like a giant cucumber! I wonder how tall it is?"

"I'd say about 180 metres tall," said the man. "Some people think it looks like a cucumber. Some people would even say it looks like a gherkin, but I think that it

definitely looks more like a giant space rocket. Now I must get on," said the man in the bright white suit.

Noah thanked the man for telling him that the office block was 180 metres tall and shaped like a space rocket. It was then that Noah realised something.

"Good heavens," cried Noah excitedly, "this is it, this is it, this is my rocket! All I have to do is to put the rocket engines into the basement without anyone noticing and then put Ethel, the kids, their wives and all the animals I have to collect into the building and blast off into orbit."

Noah then had another thought.

"The building won't fly like a rocket unless it's got fins! I'll have to fix them on just before blast-off in case people see them and get very suspicious."

Noah couldn't get home quickly enough to tell Ethel the wonderful news. It looked as though things were going to turn out right after all.

CHAPTER 5

Noah told Ethel about the office building that he had found and how the mission was definitely back on again. She, the kids and their wives were to start getting packed to be ready for the journey into space. Ethel thought it was pointless arguing any more. Noah was very determined to do what he had been told to do and anyway, Ethel thought, as they had not had a holiday for a long time, it might not be a bad idea after all. As for all the animals that were going along with them, Ethel had always wondered what it would be like to tickle a gorilla, blow soap bubbles at a giraffe, or dance with a penguin.

By now, Noah had thought of a plan for secretly putting the rocket engines into the office block. In the middle of the night, he set off in his car with the engines strapped onto the roof. Soon he arrived at the office block. But sitting in the entrance hall of the office block was a man in a white uniform.

"How am I going to get past the night security guard?" thought Noah.

The security guard had noticed Noah's car parked outside the building. He got up out of his seat in the entrance hall, opened the front door, and came over to Noah's car.

"That's it, I've had it now," thought Noah. "This is where my wonderful plan will come to nothing."

"Good evening sir," said the security guard, "can I help you?"

Noah thought that he must tell the truth.

"Actually" said Noah, "would you mind if I take these giant rocket engines into your building? I need to fix them into the basement."

"Not a problem sir" said the security guard. "It makes a nice change from people wanting to get past me into the building just because they want to steal something. It's not every night someone asks to put two giant rocket engines into the basement. Get on with it Noah, I promise I won't say a word to anybody."

Noah was very surprised and delighted that the security guard allowed him to do what he wanted to do – so he got on with it!

Noah finished the job he had to do, thanked the security guard, got into his car and drove home.

As Noah drove home very tired but very happy he thought about the security guard.

"What a nice man, and how smart he looked in his bright white uniform. I wonder how he knew my name is Noah."

CHAPTER 6

Noah arrived home and told Ethel what had happened.

Now the rocket was ready for the launch date. He told her to get everybody to meet at the office block in the city in exactly two week's time. While everyone was getting prepared, Noah had to think very quickly about how he was going to get a male and female of all the animals in the world. Suddenly, there was a loud knock at the door. Noah opened the door to find a man in a very bright white suit.

"Good morning sir, I represent the Wizzo Computer Company, and we are offering you a trial loan of a computer for a week – how about that!"

Noah told the man that he didn't need a computer and anyway, he was going on a long holiday very soon. But the man was not going to be put off.

"Let me plug in the computer for you, I'll show you how to work it and how to get on to the Internet – it's just fantastic, you've just got to see it."

Noah let the man into his home.

"No harm in it" thought Noah, "and anyway, every time I meet a man wearing a bright white suit, something good seems to happen!"

The man set the computer up and called to Noah.

"I've got you connected to the Internet. I'll pick out any old web site to let you see how it works."

Noah looked over the man's shoulder at the screen and up popped '*The Largest Pet Shop in the World.*' web site. Noah read on.

'*We can supply any living creature, male or female. Just place your order, and we will deliver you the animals of your choice to any address in the world. Why not surprise your wife with a pair of fruit bats for her birthday*!'

"There you are Noah," said the man. "I told you it was great didn't I, and look Noah, they've got a very special offer on this week. Well, must be going."

Noah opened the front door for the man. Just then, there was a mighty clap of thunder. It began to rain very heavily.

"Looks like this storm is going to last quite a while!" said the computer salesman. "Probably forty days at a guess."

Noah then knew the time for blast off was going to be very soon. Noah became very worried again.

"How am I going to collect all the animals in time?" he thought.

He went back to look at the computer. Then he noticed The Largest Pet Shop in the World's very special offer. *'This week only, with every order for a male animal, you get a female animal absolutely free!'*

Noah realised that this was how he could get all the animals he needed very quickly. Noah did a little dance of delight before beginning the very long job of ordering all the animals from *'The Largest Pet Shop in the World.'*

After two days, Noah had ordered one of every male animal in the world and with them, the free gift of the same female animal. He also ordered enough food to last the journey for both the animals and the family. Noah thought that he should order some fish tanks, birdcages, 100 tons of hay, and two squeaky plastic dog bones. All to be delivered to the office block in the city in exactly twelve days time and on the stroke of midnight.

Noah got on with helping Ethel prepare for the trip. Ethel had also been very busy knitting woolly space suits for everyone.

"Do you think I should knit a pair of space suits for the two dogs just in case they need to be taken for a space walk?" asked Ethel.

"Not a bad idea Ethel," replied Noah. "Anyway, I've got to build

the control panel for the rocket –
won't take long, just have to
connect it up to the engines when
we get inside the office building.
Then, Ethel, if all goes well, we
blast off into space."

Ethel remembered that she
should leave a note for the
milkman.

CHAPTER 7

The day for blast-off came. Noah, Ethel, their sons and their wives met at the office block just before midnight.

Noah's first task was to fix the rocket fins onto the bottom of the building.

"Hope the animals get here on time," thought Noah.

He had just finished putting on the last fin when suddenly there was a loud roar. Around the corner came the first lorry followed by another lorry, and another and another. The driver of the first lorry got out and spoke to Noah.

"Are you Noah?" asked the lorry driver.

"I am," replied Noah.

"Sign here please – where do you want all these animals?"

"We are putting them into this office block," replied Noah.

"Fine," said the driver, "let's get on with it then."

The first animals came off the lorry and Noah guided them to the front entrance of the office block. Noah opened the door, but to his surprise, the security guard with the white uniform wasn't there. Instead, there sat a different security guard dressed in a black

uniform. The man got out of his seat to see what was going on and was nearly knocked to the ground by a pair of gorillas followed quickly by a pair of sea lions. "Oy! What do you think you are doing?" he shouted to Noah.

"You can't bring your gorillas in here - it's not allowed - and get the rest of these animals out of here or I'll get the police."

Noah, helped by Ben, Joseph, and David, was too busy getting all the animals into the building to take any notice of the security guard. Two eagles flew in and knocked the security guard's hat off.

"That does it," said the security guard, "I'm off to get a policeman."

Before too long, Noah had got all the animals, all the supplies, Ethel and the rest of the family into the building. He closed the front doors then shouted across to Ethel.

"Take the lift to the top floor. I'm going to connect the wires to the engines and bring the control panel up to the top floor office. See you there."

Noah connected the wires from the engines to the control panel and took the lift to the top floor.

"Right," said Noah. "No point in waiting any longer. That security guard may come back with a policeman. Let's blast off now-everyone put on your woolly space suits."

"Can I do the countdown?" asked Ethel.

"Of course you can," said Noah. "In fact, let's all do it!"

So Noah, Ethel their sons and their wives all shouted out together:

"TEN, NINE, EIGHT, SEVEN, SIX, FIVE, FOUR, THREE, TWO, ONE,

BLAST OFF!!"

The powerful rocket engines roared into life. The office block broke free from the ground and started to slowly rise up into the night sky. Then, with a burst of speed, the rocket disappeared up beyond the clouds on its way into space.

Meanwhile, back on the ground, the security guard finally found a policeman.

"Come quickly," said the security guard. "A man and seven other people forced their way into my office block – you know, the one that looks like a giant cucumber. Not only that, he's brought hundreds and hundreds of animals with him, and he's put them all into my building."

"Calm down sir," said the policeman. "You are telling me that a man has put hundreds of animals into your building - now why would he want to do a ridiculous thing like that?"

"If you don't believe me, come back with me now to the office block and I'll show you," said the security guard.

The policeman followed the security guard back to the building. Turning the corner, the security guard suddenly stopped and stared.

"It's gone! The building's gone!" cried the security guard. "It was here five minutes ago, I know it was, I know it was. I must be going potty. What am I going to tell the boss when he comes in to work in the morning?"

"Best report this to the police station," said the policeman. "Can you give me a description of the building?"

Soon the call went out. "Calling all cars, calling all cars. Watch out for a tall office block shaped like a giant cucumber. Reported stolen at 2a.m. this morning by eight people and hundreds of animals."

CHAPTER 8

Noah's rocket was now in space and orbiting around the Earth.

"I'd better take a look down below to see if the animals are alright," said Noah.

He opened the door to the control room office and had to duck his head back in very quickly as an elephant was floating past the door.

"Weightlessness – I'd forgotten about that," said Noah.

"Well I didn't," said Ethel. "You and I, and the rest of the family aren't floating around because I knitted us some heavy woolly boots."

"Well you'd better knit a few more for some of the animals," said Noah. "I'm sure some of them aren't happy floating around all over the place."

Noah tried again to get out of the office door to check on the animals. This time, only a pair of kangaroos was floating down the corridor. Noah got into the lift and checked every floor. All the animals seemed to be fine even though all of them were floating around everywhere. He took the lift back to the control office.

"A bit chaotic down there," said Noah, "but they all seem fine."

Then Noah heard a lot of barking at the door. He opened it to find two dogs.

"See, I told you it was a good idea to knit the dogs some space suits. Now you can do what they want you to do," said Ethel.

"You mean take them out for a space walk?" said Noah.

"Exactly," said Ethel. "Pop their space suits on, twice around the rocket – I'll have your tea ready by the time you get back."

Noah opened a window, and climbed out of the rocket. Ethel handed him the two dogs and off they went.

Half an hour later, they were back.

"Nice walk?" asked Ethel.

"Not bad," replied Noah. "I suppose the dogs will want to go for a walk every night now – it's a good job I don't need to take the fish out for a swim!"

"Very funny," said Ethel. "But I hope we can go back to Earth soon before all the other animals start wanting to do what they usually do - then there'll be trouble Noah."

"You could be right," said Noah. "I wonder how long it will be before we'll be able to go back."

CHAPTER 9

Just when Noah was thinking that life on board the rocket was getting a little boring, he heard the sound of laughter that seemed to be coming from the floor below.

"What's going on down there Joseph?" he asked his son.

"It's Mum, she decided to go and tickle a gorilla."

"Well I hope she doesn't tickle an elephant or a whale, the noise will be terrible! What are the others up to?"

Joseph told Noah that Ben had gone down twenty floors to

organise a football match between the creepy crawlies and the winged insects.

"I hope you're not going to tell me the old joke about the centipede delaying the start of the match because it took hours to put on all of his football boots."

"I'm afraid to say, that is exactly what happened," said Joseph. "Anyway, I'm going to go down and join David who is organising a talent contest – last I heard he had got quite a few entries. We have a rabbit magician who promises a great trick by pulling a hat out of the other rabbit's ear, a singing tiger, a monkey who does a trapeze act, and a musical double act - a giraffe who plays the piano for a fish who plays the violin."

"Sounds like good fun," laughed Noah.

Joseph left the top floor control centre to join David, and Ethel came back from tickling the gorilla. Noah was wondering what wonderful games he could play with some of the animals.

"What would it be like to make friends with the hedgehogs and have a game of spot the leopard with them?"

"Had enough?" he asked.

"Certainly not," said Ethel, "I'm off to have a dance with a penguin."

"Don't tread on his webbed feet," said Noah.

It seemed everyone on board was very busy keeping the animals happy and having a lot of fun doing it as well!

CHAPTER 10

After 140 days of whizzing around the earth in the rocket, Noah was beginning to wonder how he was going to know that everything would be safe back on Earth and how was he going to find out. Then he thought of a great idea.

"I'll get one of the spiders to spin a thread and lower itself from the rocket down to Earth. If the water has gone down, the spider will be able to pick up something and bring it back up to the rocket. Then I'll know that things will be back to normal and it will be safe to go back."

He told Ethel about his plan.

"I'll have to knit the spider an especially thick woolly space suit for protection if he's going down to Earth and back – I'll knit him a nice bright red suit," said Ethel. "Shouldn't take long, spiders aren't that big."

"Don't forget to knit eight legs on the space suit," said Noah.

Noah then went down three floors to the room where the two spiders were.

He opened the door of the room and called out, "I'm looking for a very brave, down to earth spider," said Noah.

The male spider walked forward as if to say "I'm spider enough for the job!"

"Good lad," said Noah, "come with me."

He took the spider back up to the control room and showed him to Ethel.

"What a brave little spider," she said. "He's quite cute as well! I'm going to give him a name – how about . . . Stanley?"

Noah agreed. "Mr. Spider, you will now be known as Stanley.

Now then young Stanley, pop on your woolly space suit."

Stanley put on his eight – legged space suit. Ethel thought she had knitted the eighth leg a bit too long.

"No time for alterations now," said Noah, "the space suit is just fine."

Noah opened the window and let Stanley out. Attaching his silky thread to the rocket, Stanley began to lower himself down to Earth. Stanley spun down through the very dark blue of space lit by thousands of stars. He could see the Earth below him, covered in fluffy white clouds. As he got closer, Stanley broke through the clouds and, as he got closer, he saw that there was nothing but water. With nothing to pick up as a sign that things were back to normal, Stanley began climbing back up to the rocket.

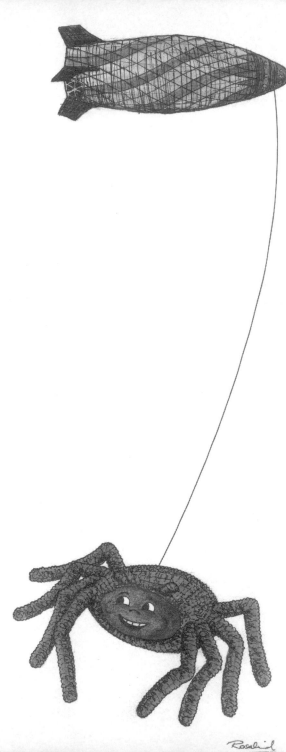

Back on board the rocket, Noah was looking out of the window when up popped something wearing a bright red woolly space suit and waving all eight legs. It was Stanley. Noah opened the window and helped him back inside the rocket. He saw that he had brought back absolutely nothing.

"Looks like things are not back to normal on Earth just yet," said Noah. "We'll send him back down again tomorrow. He may as well stay up here in the control room with us until then."

Stanley, still wearing his woolly space suit, was so tired after his trip to Earth and back, that he

curled up in a corner and was soon
fast asleep.

CHAPTER 11

The next morning, Noah once again opened the window and let Stanley out to begin the second trip down to Earth. Just as before, Stanley lowered himself down to earth on his thread. But as he got lower and lower, he saw that the flood had gone. Not only that, Stanley saw that he was heading down towards a city.

Stanley finally landed on top of a tall lamppost. He tied his thread around the top of the lamppost, ran down it and on to the street. There were lots and lots of people walking around the city. Stanley was very happy to see this because he knew things were back to normal and all he had to do now was to find an everyday object to take back to the rocket.

As Stanley was running around the pavement trying to find something, he suddenly felt a pair of hands around his body that were lifting him up from the pavement. Stanley struggled to get free but the man who had picked him up had a very good hold on him.

"You're a cute little spider, aren't you," said the man. "And a very unusual one. I've never seen a woolly red spider before. I think you need special care and a good home to go to. I'll take you to a pet shop for safe keeping."

The man took Stanley around the corner and into the first pet shop he found.

"Good morning" said the man. "I wonder if you could find a good home for this very unusual woolly red spider."

The pet shop owner brought out a cage and told the man to pop the spider into it. The man dropped Stanley into the cage. The pet shop owner took a very close look.

"You're right," he said, "he is a very unusual spider and I will put him in the shop window to see if anyone would like to take him home and keep him as a very special pet."

The pet shop owner thanked the man and straight away put the cage with Stanley into the shop window along with a notice that read: *'Wanted a good home for this very rare woolly red spider.'*

Stanley stared through the bars of the cage and was very miserable and very worried. "How am I going to get back to the rocket?" he thought. "Somehow, I must escape from this cage, but how?"

CHAPTER 12

It was not very long before a lady had noticed Stanley in the window of the pet shop.

She decided that she would like to take Stanley home as a pet. Walking into the shop the lady told the pet shop owner that she could offer a good home to the woolly red spider in the window.

"Certainly Madam, I'll get him for you," said the shop owner.

Stanley's cage was taken out of the window and put onto the shop counter.

"He's a cute little spider alright, but he doesn't look very happy." said the lady.

"Probably missing his home in the rain forest," replied the shop owner. "I'm sure he will be happy when he finds that he is going to a good home."

"Thank you," said the lady. She picked up the cage and took it back to her house.

After a few days, Stanley was still feeling very miserable.

"You are still an unhappy little spider aren't you?" said the lady. "Even though I've given you a special treat for dinner, a nice bluebottle fly pie. I'm going to take you to see the vet to find out what is making you so unhappy."

The lady took the cage and left her house to catch a bus to the vet.

A bus soon came along and the lady got on and sat by the window with the cage on her lap. At the next stop, another lady got onto the bus and sat down beside her. After a while, the lady said to Stanley's owner,

"That looks like a cute little spider."

"Yes, he is," replied Stanley's owner. "I'm taking him to the vet because he's off his food and doesn't seem very happy."

"Could I stroke him?" asked the lady.

"Yes, if you like."

She handed the cage over to the lady who opened the lid of the cage, put her hand inside and began to gently stroke Stanley.

Stanley saw his chance for escape. Quick as a flash, he ran up the lady's hand and out of the cage. He dropped onto the floor of the bus and, putting on a very fierce look, ran up and down the bus.

Everyone on the bus jumped up and started to scream. "Stop the bus Mr. Driver, there's a large red woolly spider running loose and we want to get off." The bus stopped, the doors opened and with Stanley chasing them from the back of the bus, everybody rushed to get out. Stanley noticed that in the rush to get off the bus, one of the terrified passengers had left a mobile phone on one of the seats. "Just what I need to take back to the rocket as a sign that things are back to normal down here!" thought Stanley.

Stanley picked up the phone with his legs and got off the bus.

Stanley made his way through the streets. Soon he was back at the lamppost. He began his climb back up. It was difficult having to carry the mobile phone as well, but Stanley made it to the top, fixed on his thread, and began his climb back up to the rocket.

CHAPTER 13

Meanwhile, back on board the rocket, Noah and everyone else was very worried.

"Stanley should have been back by now," said Noah. "Something terrible must have happened to him. Do you think we should send the lady spider down to see if she can find him?"

Ethel thought it was not a bad idea. Suddenly, there was a sound they all wanted to hear – the sound of eight legs tapping on the window.

"It's Stanley!" cried Noah. "He's back!"

Everyone rushed to the window to greet the safe return of the little hero. Noah pulled him back in through the window, and saw straight away that Stanley was holding something with two of his legs.

"Ethel, look!" shouted Noah. "Stanley has brought back a mobile phone"

Then Noah heard a sound he hadn't heard for quite a while – the mobile phone started to ring!

"Better answer it," said Ethel.

Noah pressed the button.

"HELLO, IS THAT YOU NOAH?" said the voice.

Noah said that it was. He knew straight away that it was God.

"THE TIME HAS COME FOR YOU TO GO BACK TO EARTH.

ALL THE HORRIBLE PEOPLE HAVE GONE.

I HAVE CHOSEN YOU TO TRY AND MAKE SURE THAT FROM NOW ON, PEOPLE ARE VERY KIND AND PLEASANT TO ONE ANOTHER. WE DON'T WANT ANY MORE HORRIBLE PEOPLE DO WE NOAH?

THIS IS MY COMMANDMENT TO YOU."

The phone went quiet.

Noah told Ethel what God had told him to try and do.

"That's quite a big job he has given you," said Ethel. "You had better make sure you do as you're told and don't get it wrong because you won't get me up in this thing again!"

"I will do my best." replied Noah.

"Now, get everyone ready. Ethel, I must set the controls for Earth. We're going home at last!"

CHAPTER 14

Noah set the controls to land the rocket in exactly the same place from where it had blasted off. With a loud roar of the rocket engines, the rocket sped back to Earth.

Floating down through the clouds, the rocket turned upside down.

"Ohhh I don't like this bit," said Ethel.

"Don't worry, it won't take long," said Noah.

And, soon enough, the rocket landed back on the ground, the

right way up. Noah and everybody else went down to the ground floor and Noah opened up the front door onto the street.

Then Noah saw five people.

All were wearing very bright white suits.

He soon recognised them: The salesman who gave him the rocket engines; the policeman who freed him from the police station; the man he bumped into when he was looking up at the office block who told him it looked like a space rocket, and the security guard who had let him put the rocket engines into the building. Finally, there was the computer salesman.

"Well done, Noah," they all said.

Just then, Ethel called to Noah to ask if she should let all the animals out.

"Definitely," said Noah.

Ethel opened the doors in the building and all the animals came out. What a grand and noisy procession it was.

Leading the procession was Stanley. There was a special cheer for him from the people in the bright white suits.

"Hurrah for Stanley!" they cheered.

All the other animals followed Stanley out of the rocket. The elephants were trumpeting, the hyenas were laughing, the monkeys were screeching, the

lions were roaring, in fact every animal made its own noise in celebration. Ben and Joseph and David carried the fish tanks down to the river and emptied them there so that the fish could all swim back to their homes.

"I wouldn't want to be the office cleaners for that building," thought Ethel as she joined Noah.

But Noah thought the right thing to do was for all the family to clean and tidy up the rocket before going home.

It wasn't long before they had finished the job and the family left the rocket for the last time.

Ethel closed the front doors. Noah's last task was to take off the rocket fins.

Then Ethel remembered something.

"Noah, who were those people in white suits you were talking to when we first came out of the rocket, and where have they gone to?" she asked.

"I don't know Ethel. But I do know that if it wasn't for those five very nice people who helped me along the way, I don't think I could have done the job."

"You know something Noah," said Ethel, "if those men helped you so much, and they all wore bright white suits and uniforms, then they must be angels!"

"You know something, Ethel," said Noah, "I think you are absolutely right!"

Then Ethel saw something in the sky.

"Look over there Noah – in the sky" shouted Ethel. "What a big rainbow!"

Noah turned around to look at the most amazing rainbow he had ever seen.

They both just stood there looking at the amazing rainbow.

After a while, Noah realised something.

"Ethel?" said Noah, "If you look at a rainbow upside down, it looks like a giant smile!"

"Well, you know what they say don't you?" said Ethel. "Turn that frown upside down!"

Noah laughed. Ethel then

thought that Noah should put up a little sign next to the office building saying '*Noah's Rocket*' so people would know that this is where it all happened. But Noah was thinking about his little hero, Stanley.

"I wonder how he is getting on and where he is now?"

Then he turned to Ethel and told her that the next time he saw a spider, he would look very closely to see if it was Stanley.

"You're sure to recognize him," said Ethel. "If he's forgotten to take it off, he could be the only spider you will ever see wearing a red woolly space suit!"

"It wouldn't surprise me," said Noah, "You're still wearing yours Ethel!"

"Lets get home now," he said. "I've got some important work to do. I've got to start helping to make the world a better place."

Soon, Noah and Ethel had arrived back at their house.

"It's as if we had never been away," said Ethel, "Nothing seems to have changed."

"Oh but things are going to be different," said Noah.

Straight away, he went to see his next-door neighbour, the one who had called the police to stop Noah building his rocket.

Noah knocked on the door.

"Hello Noah," said the neighbour, "how are you? Have you been away?"

"Yes I have," said Noah, "but I'm back to say I'm very sorry to have caused you all that trouble because of the rocket."

"That's alright Noah," said the neighbour. "I'm sorry that I also gave you a bit of trouble."

The two men smiled and shook hands. Noah turned to go back home, very happy that he had done his first good deed by being polite and that the neighbour had been very polite in return.

Noah was certain that he was going to succeed in carrying out God's commands.